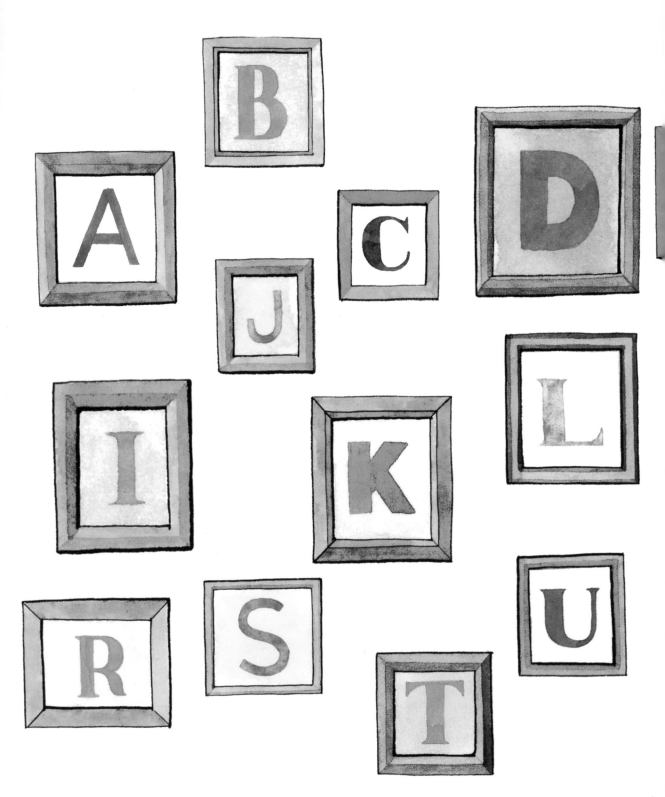

MADALENA MONIZ

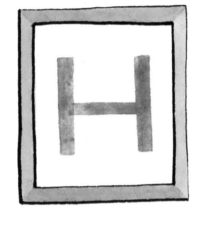

An Alphabet of Feelings

Abrams Appleseed, New York

Adored

Brilliant

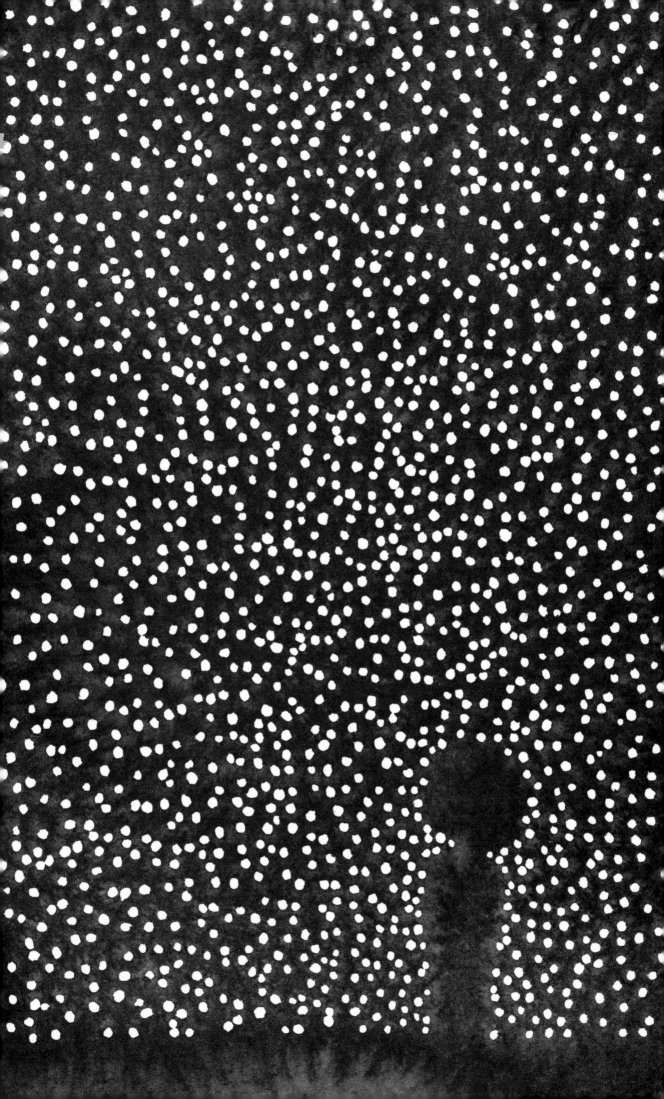

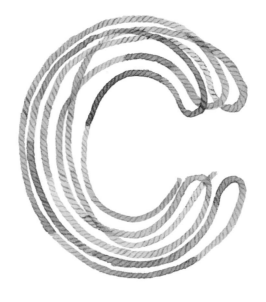

Curious

Daring

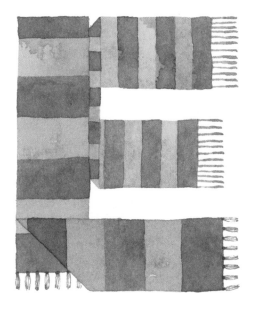

Excited

Free

Grumpy

Heroic

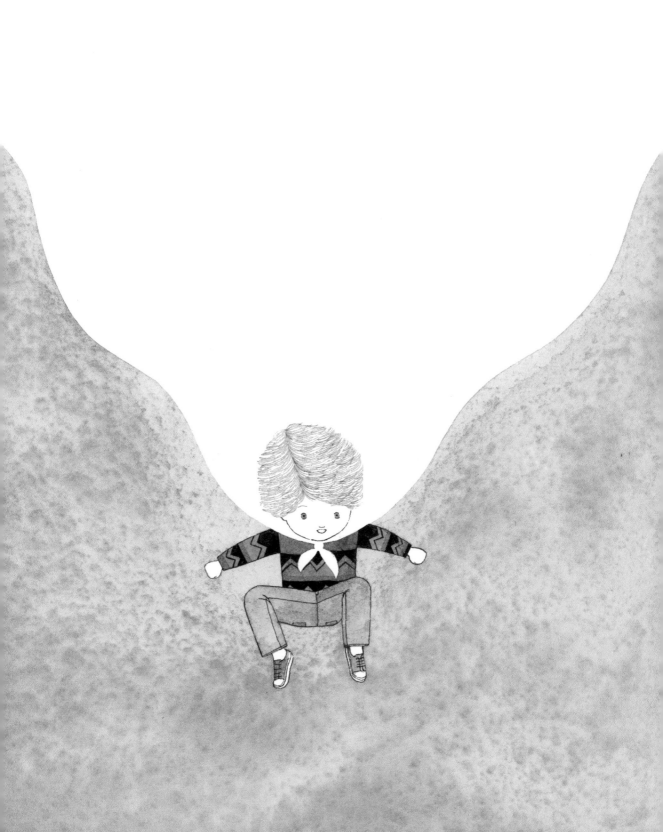

Invisible

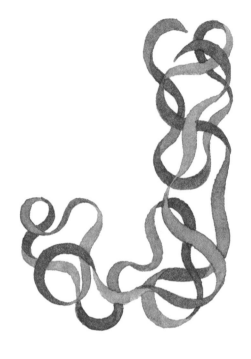

Jealous

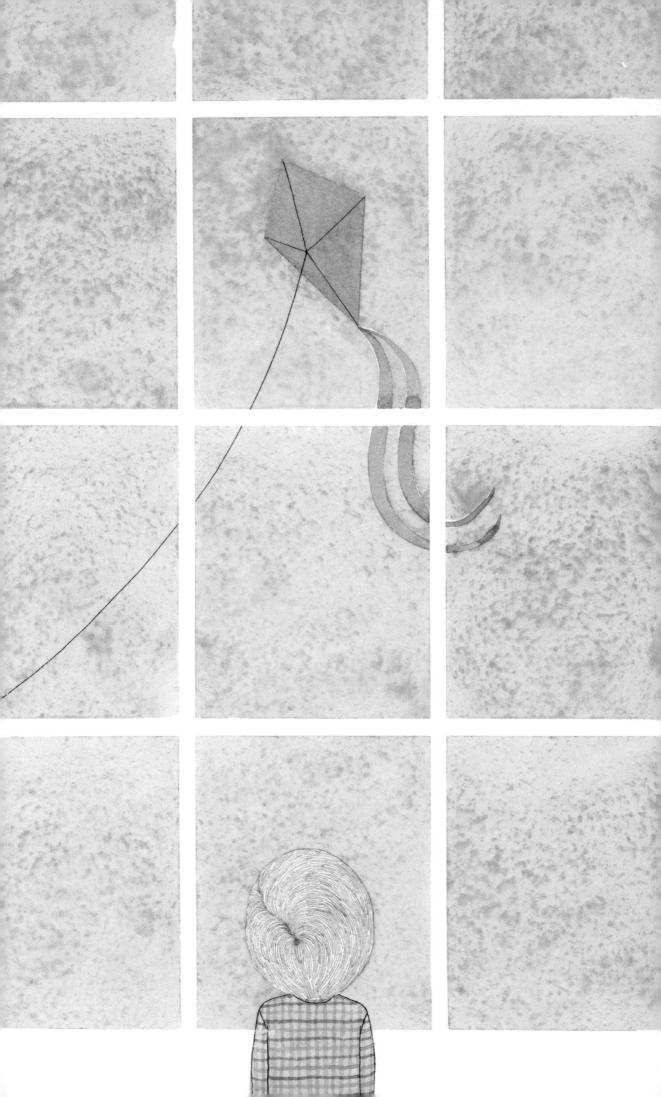

Kind

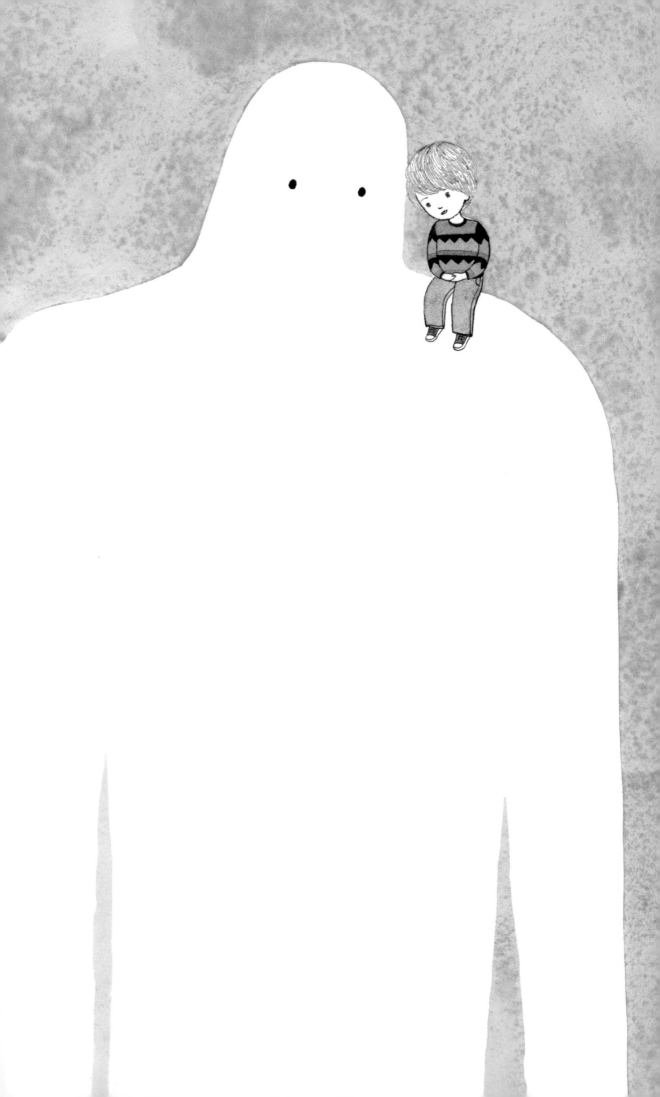

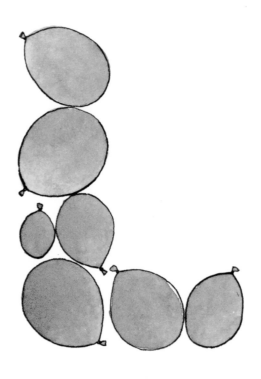

Light

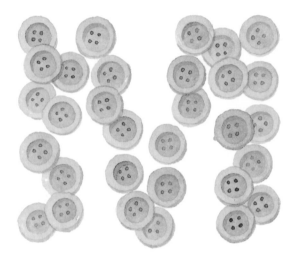

Mini

Nervous

Original

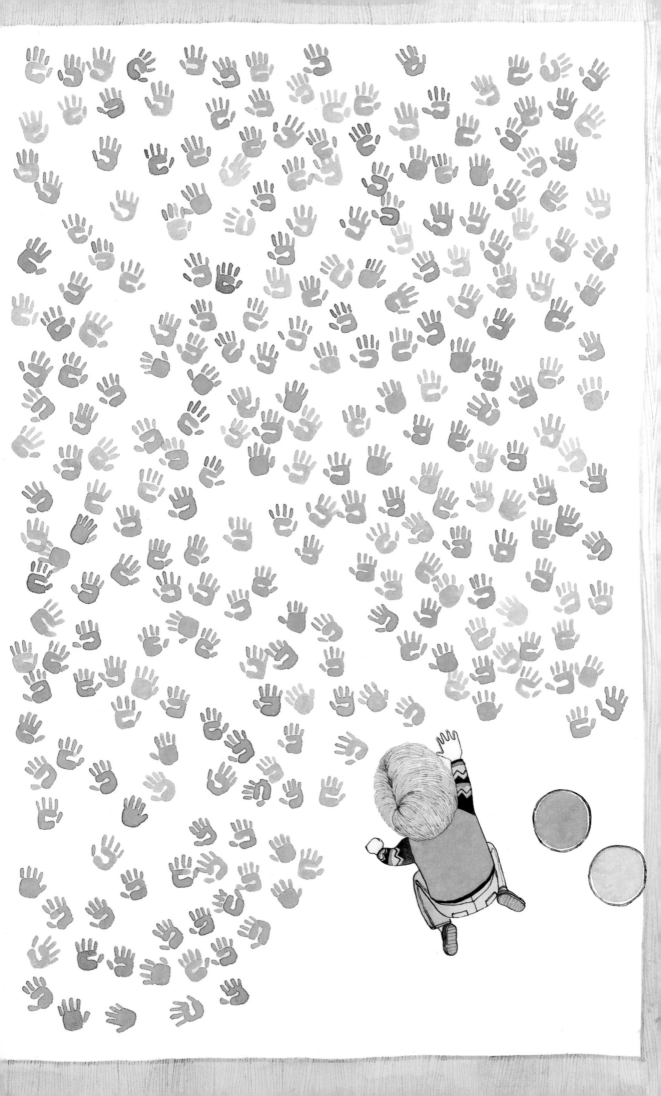

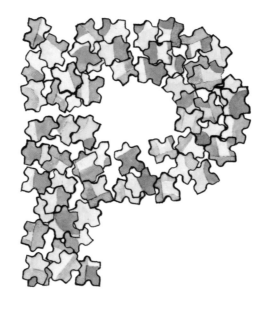

Patient

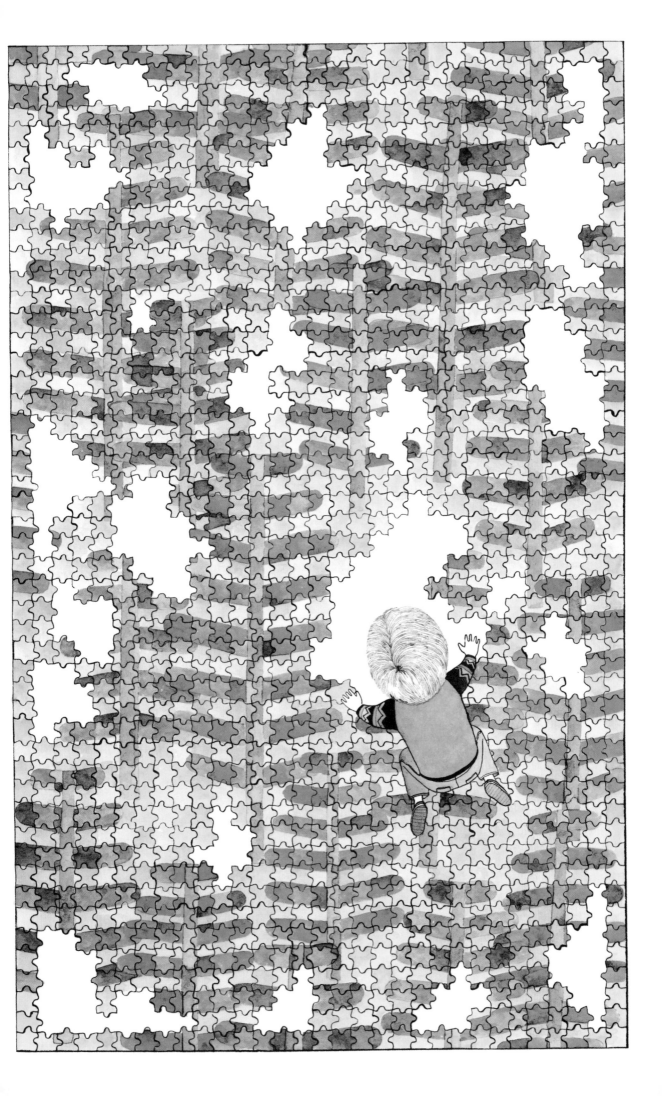

Quiet

Relaxed

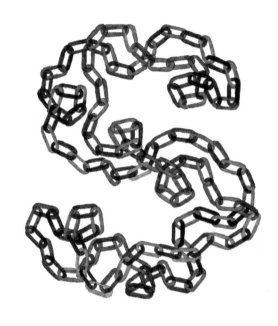

Strong

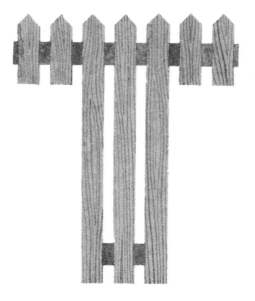

Tall

Uncertain

Victorious

Warm

X.O.X.O.'ed

Yucky

Zzzz

HOW DO YOU FEEL TODAY?

**For my parents and brother
—MM**

The illustrations in this book were made with watercolor and india ink.

Cataloging-in-Publication Data has been applied for and may be obtained from
the Library of Congress.

ISBN: 978-1-4197-2324-7

Printed and bound in China
10 9 8 7 6 5 4 3 2 1

For bulk discount inquiries, contact specialsales@abramsbooks.com.

ABRAMS The Art of Books
115 West 18th Street, New York, NY 10011
abramsbooks.com